MARY HOF...   : range from

picture boo...   ...aturing the

feisty and...   ...l acclaim

and sold...   ...ooks for

Frances Lin...   *...Like Me* and

Kings and ...   *...of Families*,

which won th...   ...ward in 2011,

and *The ...*   ...s Asquith.

Mary lives i...   ...urmese cats.

Sh...   ...ts.

CAROL...   ...ator of

Please renew or return items by the date
shown on your receipt

www.hertfordshire.gov.uk/libraries

Renewals and enquiries: 0300 123 4049

Textphone for hearing or 0300 123 4041
speech impaired users:

L32 11.16

Hertfordshire

Amazing Grace and *Starring Grace* by Mary Hoffman,
and *Down by the River* by Grace Hallworth. She wrote and illustrated
the picture books *Gregory Cool*, *Since Dad Left*, *New Born*, *Silver Shoes*
and *Cristy's Dream*, as well as one novel for young readers about
a traveller family, *Road Horse*. Caroline lives in Cornwall.

D0183346

Quarto is the authority on a wide range of topics.

Quarto educates, entertains and enriches the lives of our readers—enthusiasts and lovers of hands-on living.

www.quartoknows.com

For Sue Lubeck, who couldn't wait – M.H.

For Taj and all the Mahals:
"Families are what you make them." – C.B.

Text copyright © Mary Hoffman 1995
Illustrations copyright © Caroline Binch 1995

First published in Great Britain in 1995 by
Frances Lincoln Children's Books, The Old Brewery,
6 Blundell Street, London, N7 9BH, UK
www.franceslincoln.com

This paperback edition published in 2007

All rights reserved

No part of this publication may be reproduced, stored in a retrieval system,
or transmitted, in any form, or by any means, electrical, mechanical,
photocopying, recording or otherwise without the prior written permission of
the publisher or a licence permitting restricted copying. In the United Kingdom
such licences are issued by the Copyright Licensing Agency,
Saffron House, 6-10 Kirby Street, London ECIN 8TS.

A Catalogue record for this book is available from the British Library

ISBN 978-1-84507-806-5

Manufactured in Shenzhen, China RD092017

18

Grace
& family

Mary Hoffman
Illustrated by Caroline Binch

F

FRANCES LINCOLN
CHILDREN'S BOOKS

Grace lived with her Ma and her Nana and a cat called Paw-Paw. Next to her family, what Grace liked best was stories. Some she knew and some she made up, and she was particularly interested in ones about fathers, because she didn't have one.

"You do too have a father," her Ma said when she caught Grace talking that way. "I must have told you a hundred times about how we split up and your Papa went back to Africa. He has another family now, but he's still your father, even though he doesn't live with us any more."

Well, that wasn't Grace's idea of a father! She wanted one like Beauty's, who brought her roses from the Beast's garden in spite of the dangers. Not one she hadn't seen since she was very little and only knew from letters and photographs.

And in her school reading books Grace saw that all the families had a mother and a father, a boy and a girl, and a dog and a cat.

"Our family's not right," she told Nana. "We need a father and a brother and a dog."

"Well," said Nana, "I'm not sure how Paw-Paw would feel about a dog. And what about me? Are there any Nanas in your school book?"

Grace shook her head.

"So do you want me to go?" asked Nana, smiling.

"Of course not!" Grace said, hugging her. Nana hugged her back.

"Families are what you make them," she said.

Then, one day when Grace got in from school she saw a letter on the table with a crocodile stamp on it. Grace knew it must be from Papa, but it wasn't Christmas or her birthday.

Ma said, "Guess what! Your Papa sent the money for two tickets to visit him in Africa for the Easter holidays. Nana says she'll go with you if you want. What do you say?"

But Grace was speechless. She had made up so many fathers for herself she had forgotten what the real one was like.

Grace and Nana left for Africa on a very cold grey day.
They arrived in The Gambia in golden sunshine like
the hottest summer back home. It had been a long, long
journey. Grace barely noticed the strange sights and
sounds that greeted her. She was thinking of Papa.

"I wonder if he will still love me?" thought Grace.
"He has other children now and in stories it's always
the youngest that is the favourite." She held on tightly
to Nana.

Outside the airport was a man who looked a little like Papa's photo. He swung Grace up in his arms and held her close. Grace buried her nose in his shirt and thought, "I do remember."

In the car she started to notice how different everything seemed. There were sheep wandering along the roadside and people selling watermelons under the trees.

And when they reached her father's compound, there was the biggest difference of all. A pretty young woman with a little girl and a baby boy came to meet them. Grace said hello but couldn't manage another word all evening. Everyone thought she was just tired. Except Nana.

"What's the matter, honey?" she asked when they went to bed. "You've got a father and a brother now and they even have a dog!"

But Grace thought, "They make a storybook family without me. I'm one girl too many. Besides, it's the wrong Ma."

The next day, Grace started to get to know Neneh and
Bakary. The children thought it was wonderful to have
a big sister all the way from England. And Grace
couldn't help liking them too. But she had to feel cross
with someone.

Grace knew lots of stories about wicked stepmothers –
Cinderella, Snow White, Hansel and Gretel – so she
decided to be cross with Jatou. "I won't clean the house
for her," thought Grace, "I won't eat anything she cooks
and I won't let her take me into the forest."

Jatou made a big dish of savoury benachim for lunch, but Grace wouldn't eat any. "I'm not hungry," she said.

"She's probably still getting over the long flight," said Jatou.

When Papa came home from work, he found Grace in the backyard. He sat beside her under the big old jackfruit tree.

"This is where my grandma used to tell me stories when I was a little boy," he said.

"Nana tells me stories too," said Grace.

"Did she ever tell you the one about how your Ma and I came to split up?" asked Papa.

"I know that one," said Grace, "but I don't want to hear it right now," and she covered up her ears.

Papa hugged her. "Would you like the one about the Papa who loved his little girl so much he saved up all his money to bring her to visit him?"

"Yes, I'd like that one," said Grace.

"OK. But if I tell you that story, will you promise me to try to be nice to Jatou? You're both very important to me," said Papa.

Grace thought about it. "I'll try," she said.

Next day, they went to the food market. It was much more exciting than shopping at home. Even the money had crocodiles on it! Lots of the women carried their shopping on their heads.

Then they went to a stall which was like stepping
inside a rainbow. There was cloth with crocodiles
and elephants on it and cloth with patterns made
from pebbles and shells. And so many colours!

"We can choose cloth for Grace's first African dress," said Papa. Grace and Nana spent a long time choosing. No one was in a hurry.

The days of Grace's visit flew by. She played in the
ocean with her brother and sister, and she told them
a bedtime story every night. She told all the stories she
knew – Beauty and the Beast, Rapunzel, Rumpelstiltskin.
It was amazing how many stories were about fathers
who gave their daughters away. But she didn't tell
them any about wicked stepmothers.

Sometimes Ma rang up from home, and then Grace felt strange. "I feel like gum stretched out all thin in a bubble," she told Nana. "As if there isn't enough of me to go round. I can't manage two families. What if I burst?"

"Families are what you make them," said Nana. "A family with you in it is your family."

Soon it was their last evening and there was a big farewell party at the compound. Grace and Nana wore their African clothes and Grace ate twice as much benachim as everyone else.

"Now you really might burst," said Nana.

But Grace wasn't worried about bursting any more.
She just wanted to dance with her African family.

On their last morning, Papa took Grace
to see some real crocodiles. "This is a special
holy place," he said. "The crocodiles are so tame
you can stroke them."

"Not like the one in Peter Pan!" said Grace.

"No, these are so special you can make a wish
on them," said Papa.

Grace closed her eyes and made a wish, but she
wouldn't say what it was.

Later at the compound, Grace asked Nana, "Why aren't there any stories about families like mine, that don't live together?"

"Well at least you've stopped thinking it's your family that's wrong," said Nana. "Now all you have to do is make up a new story to go with it."

"I'll do that," said Grace, "and when we're home again, I'll write it down and send it to Jatou to read to Neneh and Bakary."

The whole family came to see them off at the airport. Grace was sorry to say goodbye to her stepmother and her new brother and sister. But leaving Papa was hardest of all.

Waiting for their plane, Nana asked Grace if she had thought any more about her story.

"Yes, but I can't think of the right ending," said Grace, "because the story's still going on."

"How about they lived happily ever after?" asked Nana

"That's a good one," said Grace. "Or they lived happily ever after, though not all in the same place."

"Stories are what you make them," said Nana.

"Just like families," said Grace.

OTHER GRACE TITLES FROM
FRANCES LINCOLN CHILDREN'S BOOKS

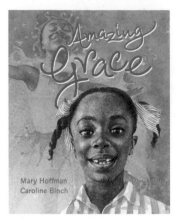

AMAZING GRACE
By Mary Hoffman
Illustrated by Caroline Binch

Grace loves to act out stories. Sometimes she plays
the leading part, sometimes she is a cast of thousands.
When her school plans a performance of *Peter Pan,*
she longs to play Peter, but her classmates say that he
was a boy, and besides, he wasn't black… But Grace's Ma
and Nana tell her she can be anything she wants if she
puts her mind to it.

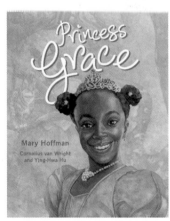

PRINCESS GRACE
By Mary Hoffman
Illustrated by Cornelius van Wright and Ying-Hwa Hu

Grace is back! The girl from Amazing Grace who proved that
you can be anything you want and that families are what
you make them, discovers that there's more than one way
to be a princess.

GRACE AT CHRISTMAS
By Mary Hoffman
Illustrated by Cornelius van Wright and Ying-Hwa Hu

Grace loves Christmas – acting out the nativity story,
opening presents, celebrating with Ma, Nana and Paw-Paw.
But this Christmas Nana announces they will have visitors
from Trinidad. Grace is horrified! She does NOT want to
share the day with another little girl she doesn't even know.
But after some wise words from Nana, Grace's generous spirit
shines through. And in the end, as they all share a special
surprise, Grace thinks it could be the best Christmas ever!

Frances Lincoln titles are available from all good bookshops.
You can also buy books and find out more about your favourite titles,
authors and illustrators on our website: www.franceslincoln.com